The Junior Novelization

randomhousekids.com

ISBN 978-0-7364-3655-7

Printed in the United States of America

10 9 8 7 6 5 4 3 2 1

DISNEY · PIXAR

FINDING NEMO

Adapted by Gail Herman

Designed by Disney's Global Design Group

Random House New York

PROLOGUE

In the warm tropical waters off the coast of Australia, two clownfish swam at the edge of the Great Barrier Reef. Here the ocean was a place of brightly colored anemones, towering corals, and delicate sea plants. But just beyond the reef was the vast open sea.

"Yes, honey. It's beautiful," a clownfish named Coral said nervously to her husband, Marlin.

"When you said you wanted an ocean view, you didn't think you were gonna get the whole ocean, did you? Oh, yeah. A fish can breathe out here," Marlin boasted.

He grinned. The edge of the Great Barrier Reef! He couldn't think of a better spot to make their new home.

"I know that the Drop-off is desirable, with the great schools and the amazing view and all that. But do we really need so much space?" Although Coral loved her new anemone home, she was a bit cautious about the location near the open sea, with its unpredictable dangers.

"Coral, honey. Our kids deserve the best," Marlin said. "They'll wake up, poke their little heads out of the window, and they'll see a whale passing right by."

"Shhh! You're gonna wake the kids," Coral whispered. They gazed inside the cozy cave just below the anemone, where hundreds of tiny fish eggs nestled close together—Marlin and Coral's children.

Marlin couldn't wait for their babies to hatch. He wanted to show his children all the sights of the glorious ocean.

"We still have to name them," Coral said.

Marlin puffed up with pride and drew an imaginary line down the center of the group of eggs with his fin. "We'll name this half Marlin junior and this half Marlene."

"I like Nemo," Coral said.

"Nemo?" Marlin repeated. "Well, we'll name one Nemo."

Coral looked over at Marlin wistfully. "Just think," she said. "In a couple of days we're going to be parents."

"What if they don't like me?" Marlin said.

"There's over four hundred eggs. Odds are one of them is bound to like you," Coral teased.

Marlin stared at her and shyly asked, "You remember how we met?"

"Well, I try not to," Coral replied.

Marlin playfully chased his wife in and out of the anemone. "I remember," he said. "'Excuse me, miss. Could you check and see if I have a hook in my lip? Oh, you gotta look closer.'"

Coral laughed and swam out of the anemone to avoid getting caught by her husband. Marlin poked his head out of the anemone and was startled to find that the neighborhood was eerily quiet. He spotted Coral, who was motionless, staring into the water at a hungry barracuda.

"Get inside the house, Coral," he whispered.

But Coral didn't want to leave her babies exposed. She darted for the grotto, but was too slow—the barracuda reached her as she entered the cave.

Marlin slammed against the barracuda, trying desperately to save his wife. But with a quick swish of its tail, the barracuda batted Marlin against some rocks. Dazed, Marlin floated down *into the protective fronds of an anemone.*

After the sand had settled, Marlin came to with a start and bolted out of the anemone.

"Coral?" he called.

There was no answer. He peered inside the grotto. Empty. He squinted into the vast blue water.

Nothing.

Coral was gone. The eggs were gone.

Marlin couldn't believe this was happening! In the space of a few minutes, his life had been changed forever. His family was gone. He shook his head. He felt like it was his fault. He shouldn't have insisted they live by the Drop-off. As he sadly turned away, he noticed something out of the corner of his eye.

Lying on a small ledge not far away was one tiny egg. It was damaged with a small scratch. But the egg was alive. Alive!

Marlin cradled the egg in his fin. "There, there. Daddy's here. And I promise, I will never let anything happen to you . . ." He paused a moment, then called the egg by name.

"Nemo."

CHAPTER 1

Deep in the ocean, the morning sun's rays shone through the water. Inside an anemone, an excited young clownfish jumped awake. "First day of school!" he shouted to his father. "Wake up! Come on!"

"I don't want to go to school," Marlin muttered.

"Not you, Dad. Me!" Nemo cried.

"Huh?" Marlin shook himself awake. "All right, I'm up. It's time for school."

"It's time for school!" Nemo repeated in a singsong voice. He'd never been to school before. He was excited about exploring the ocean with his class. Visiting different places. Trying different things!

He'd never been far from his anemone home—and he couldn't wait to see more of the ocean.

Nemo somersaulted and accidentally crashed out of the anemone. Before he knew it, he was stuck headfirst in some coral.

"Nemo!" Marlin shouted, fully awake. He raced outside.

"First day of school! First day of school!" Nemo sang in a muffled voice.

Quickly, Marlin pulled him from the coral, then tugged him inside their home.

"All right, where's the break?" he asked Nemo in an anxious voice. "Are you woozy? How many stripes do I have?"

"I'm fine." Nemo knew his dad was worried. He *always* worried.

"Answer the stripe question!" Marlin demanded.

"Three," Nemo replied.

Marlin sighed, relieved. "How's the lucky fin?"

Nemo glanced down at his fin. It was withered, a little misshapen from his encounter with the barracuda when he was still an egg. "Lucky."

"Now, are you sure you want to go to school this year?" Marlin asked. "You can wait five or six years."

No way, Nemo thought. "Dad, it's time for school!" he repeated.

Marlin looked around. What could keep Nemo home, safe and sound, if only for a few more minutes? "Aha!" he cried. "You forgot to brush!"

Brushing was very important, Nemo knew. Clownfish lived in anemone homes because the anemones' fronds were poisonous and protected the little fish from predators. Brushing up against the anemone stingers, a little bit every day, made the clownfish immune to the poison.

Nemo backed up into a tendril and brushed against it. "Okay, I'm done!" he said quickly.

"You missed a spot," said Marlin.

"Where?" Nemo asked.

"There!" Marlin tickled Nemo under a fin. "And right there." He tickled Nemo under his other fin.

Nemo giggled, and together they swam out the door.

"Dad, maybe while I'm at school I'll see a shark!" Nemo said excitedly. Then he asked, "How old are sea turtles?"

"I—I don't know," Marlin admitted.

"Sandy Plankton, from next door, said that sea turtles live to be about a hundred years old!" Nemo cried.

"Well, if I ever meet a sea turtle, I'll ask him," Marlin said.

Father and son were approaching the schoolyard now.

Two young fish tossed a shell back and forth, playing catch. "Come on, you guys! Stop it! Give that back!" a hermit crab shouted at them.

"I wonder where we're supposed to go," Marlin said, looking around. He spotted a group of fathers. "Come on. We'll try over here."

"Excuse me," Marlin said, approaching the other dads. "Is this where we meet his teacher?"

The other fish looked at him, surprised. "Well," the sea horse said, "look who's out of the anemone!" Then he turned toward a group of children playing in the nearby sand. "Sheldon!" the father called to his son. "Get out of Mr. Johannsen's yard. Now!"

The giant flounder that the small fish were playing on suddenly sprang from his resting place in the sand. The children scattered, chasing each other, playing tag.

"Dad!" Nemo whispered. "Can I go play, too?"

"I would feel better if you'd play over on the sponge beds," Marlin replied.

Nemo glanced at the soft, springy sponge beds. Little newborn fish jumped on them, their mothers watching carefully. He wasn't going over there—that was for babies!

Just then some children raced up. They were about Nemo's age. They looked at him curiously.

"What's wrong with his fin?" asked a pink octopus named Pearl.

"He looks funny," said Tad, a butterfly fish.

"Be nice," Tad's dad warned. "It's his first time at school."

"See this tentacle?" Pearl asked Nemo. "It's actually shorter than all my other tentacles, but you can't really tell."

"I'm H$_2$O intolerant," said Sheldon. *"Achoo!"*

"I'm obnoxious," said Tad.

Just then a big blue manta ray swam up to the reef. "Mr. Ray!" shouted the children, rushing over to the teacher.

"Come aboard, explorers," said Mr. Ray. The children lined up in front of their teacher. Nemo joined them, with Marlin right by his side.

Nemo turned red. "Dad, you can go now," he whispered. But Marlin stayed right where he was.

One by one, the children climbed aboard Mr. Ray.

"Well, hello," Mr. Ray said when Nemo reached him. "Who is this?"

"I'm Nemo."

"Well, Nemo, all new explorers must answer a science question," Mr. Ray said. "You live in what kind of home?"

"In an anemon-ene . . . amanemone . . . ammeneme . . . anemone," Nemo said, struggling to say the word.

"Okay, okay, don't hurt yourself," Mr. Ray said. "Welcome aboard, explorer!"

"Just so you know," Marlin added quietly, "he's got a little fin. I find if he's having trouble swimming, I let him take a break— ten, fifteen minutes—"

"Dad," Nemo said, annoyed, "it's time for you to go now!"

"Don't worry," Mr. Ray told Marlin. "We're gonna stay together as a group."

"Bye, Dad!" Nemo shouted as Mr. Ray swam away with the students.

"Bye, son!" Marlin called. "Be safe," he said to himself.

Sheldon's dad turned to Marlin. "Hey, you're doing pretty well for a first-timer."

"Well, you can't hold on to them forever, can you?" Marlin replied.

"Yeah, I had a tough time when my oldest went out on the Drop-off," Tad's dad said.

"The Drop-off?" Marlin shouted. "Why don't we just fry them up now and serve them with chips?"

Without any hesitation, he raced after Nemo.

CHAPTER 2

A few minutes later, Mr. Ray and the children arrived at the Drop-off.

"All right, kids," said Mr. Ray. "Feel free to explore. But stay close." The class gathered around Mr. Ray as he began his science lesson.

Tad turned to Pearl and Sheldon. "Come on," he whispered. "Let's go."

The three friends sneaked away from the group.

"Hey, guys. Wait up," said Nemo. He raced after them. But once he realized where he was, he stopped short. He was at the edge of the reef. The ocean spread out before him. It was so big, so wide, and so blue—it was like nothing he'd ever seen.

"Whoa!" he exclaimed.

"Cool!" said Sheldon, Pearl, and Tad at the same time.

Tad pushed Pearl toward the edge. "Aaah!" she cried. Then he yanked her back.

The small octopus looked down. She was covered in black liquid. "Aw, you guys! You made me ink!"

Nemo felt dizzy with excitement. He was playing with friends! Seeing the ocean! It was all so new.

"What's that?" Nemo pointed a fin at a dive boat floating on the surface.

"I know what it is," said Tad. "Sandy Plankton saw one. He said it was called a butt."

"Wow!" exclaimed Pearl. "That's a pretty big butt."

"Ooh-ooh, look at me," Sheldon said, starting to swim out into the open water. "I'm going to go touch the butt! *Aaaachoo!*" He sneezed, and the force of his sneeze moved him a bit closer to the boat.

"Aaah!" Sheldon screamed. He raced back to his friends.

The others laughed. "Well, let's see *you* get closer," Sheldon dared them.

Pearl jumped out, just a little past where Sheldon had been. Then she hurried back. "Beat that!"

Next Tad swam out even farther than Pearl. "Come on, Nemo!" he said. "How far can you go?"

"Oh . . . um," Nemo stammered. "My dad says it's not safe."

Suddenly, Marlin swam up next to Nemo. He pulled Nemo away from his new friends. Nervous and angry, Marlin scolded Nemo. "You were about to swim into open water!"

"No," Nemo said. "I wasn't going to go out—"

"It's just a good thing I was here," Marlin interrupted. "If I hadn't shown up—"

"But, Dad, no—" Nemo started to say.

The other children gathered around them. "Sir, he wasn't going to go," said Pearl.

"Yeah," said Tad. "He was too afraid."

"No, I wasn't!" Nemo said defensively.

"This does not concern you, kids," Marlin said to Nemo's friends. "And you're lucky I don't tell your parents you were out there!"

Then he turned to Nemo. "You know you can't swim well."

"I can swim fine, Dad, okay?" Nemo cried.

"No, it's not okay. You shouldn't be anywhere near here," Marlin said. "I was right. You know what? We'll start school in a year or two."

"No, Dad! Just because you're scared of the ocean—"

"Clearly you're not ready, and you're not coming back here till you are," Marlin said. "You think you can do these things, but you just can't, Nemo!"

"I hate you," Nemo whispered under his breath. His dad had embarrassed him in front of everyone. Nemo would show them he wasn't scared of the ocean like his dad.

"Excuse me." Mr. Ray swam up to Marlin, shooing the children away. "Is there anything I can do?"

"You know, I'm sorry. I didn't mean to interrupt things. He isn't a good swimmer, and I just think it's a little too soon for him to be out here unsupervised," Marlin explained.

"Well, I can assure you, he's quite safe with me—" Mr. Ray started to say.

Marlin shook his head, interrupting the teacher. "Look, I'm sure he is, but you have a large class. He can get lost, you know, from sight if you're not looking. Now, I'm not saying you're not looking. You're looking . . ."

As the grown-ups kept talking, one little fish gasped. "Oh my gosh! Nemo's swimming out to sea!"

"Nemo!" Marlin shouted. "What do you think you're doing? You're gonna get stuck out there, and I'm gonna have to get you before another fish does! Get back here! I said get back here, now! Stop! You take one more move, mister—"

Nemo ignored his father. *I'm getting closer,* he thought. *Closer. There!* He slapped the side of the dive boat with his fin.

"He touched the butt!" Tad said in amazement.

"You just paddle your little tail right back here, Nemo!" Marlin yelled. "That's right. You are in big trouble, young man. Do you hear me? Big—"

Marlin froze, unable to speak. But now

everyone else was shouting for Nemo to swim back quickly.

Nemo realized everyone was looking behind him. What was going on? He spun around to look. All he could see was his own reflection in a giant diver's mask. . . .

CHAPTER 3

"**D**addy! Help me!" Nemo shouted, realizing that he was in danger.

Marlin shook himself out of his daze. "Coming, Nemo!"

Mr. Ray led the other children to safety. Marlin started toward Nemo. A second diver suddenly appeared. He grabbed for Marlin. Marlin darted away, but he couldn't get around the diver. He couldn't get closer to Nemo. He could only watch as the first diver's net fell over his little son.

"No!" Marlin screamed. "Nemo!"

Nemo was being pulled to the surface of

the water . . . farther and farther away. . . .

The divers disappeared into the boat. Marlin raced toward it, but the boat's motor started and the force of the propeller pushed him back.

Still, Marlin swam with all his might. If he could just catch up . . . just get closer . . . maybe he could save Nemo.

Above the surface, the boat rocked from side to side in the choppy water. *Splash!* A diver's mask fell overboard.

Marlin swam as fast as he could in the boat's wake, but the boat sped ahead, leaving him behind. Soon it was just a speck on the horizon. And then it completely disappeared.

"Nemo! No!" Marlin shouted. He ducked underwater. "Has anybody seen a boat? Please? A white boat?" he called to a school of passing fish. "They took my son! Help me!"

No one answered. They just kept swimming, bumping into Marlin as they rushed along.

One of the fish bumped him a little too hard and he was knocked down to the ocean floor.

Dazed, Marlin looked up to see a regal blue tang fish rushing over to him.

"Oh! Sorry, I didn't see you! Sir, are you okay?" the blue tang asked.

"He's gone." Marlin groaned. "They took him away. I have to find the boat."

"A boat?" the blue tang asked. "Hey, I've seen a boat."

Marlin perked up a bit. "You have?" he asked.

"Uh-huh," the fish said. "And it passed by not too long ago."

"A white one?" Marlin asked.

The blue tang stuck out her fin and said, "Hi. I'm Dory."

"Where?" Marlin said, ignoring Dory's greeting. "Which way?"

"Oh!" said Dory. "It went this way! Follow me."

Dory led Marlin away from the reef, toward the open ocean.

"Thank you so much," said Marlin.

"No problem," Dory said, swimming along quickly.

Bit by bit, she slowed down. She glanced back at Marlin with a strange expression. Then she sped up. She swerved all around.

Is she trying to lose me? Marlin wondered.

Finally, Dory hid behind a giant plant. Marlin swam past. Then she darted out and swam the other way.

Marlin spied her and spun around, too.

"Will you quit it? I'm trying to swim here. What? The ocean isn't big enough for you?" Dory cried. "Stop following me, okay?"

Marlin was totally confused. "What are

you talking about? You're showing me which way the boat went."

Dory bobbed excitedly. "A boat? Hey, I've seen a boat. It passed by not too long ago. It—it went . . . um, this way! Follow me!"

"Wait a minute!" Marlin cried. "What is going on? You already told me which way the boat was going!"

"I did?" Dory looked embarrassed. "Oh, no! I'm so sorry. See, I suffer from short-term memory loss. I forget things almost instantly. It runs in my family. At least I think it does. Uh . . . hmm, where are they?"

She gazed into the distance, trying to remember. Then she looked at Marlin. "Can I help you?"

"You're wasting my time. I have to find my son," Marlin said.

Marlin turned tail to leave. But instead of swimming away, he could only gasp.

He was face to face with a very large shark!

CHAPTER 4

The giant shark bared row upon row of razor-sharp white teeth as its mouth spread into a wide, hungry grin.

"Hello!" said the shark.

"Well, hi!" Dory said cheerfully.

"Name's Bruce." The shark held out a fin.

Marlin shivered, too frightened to do anything.

"That's all right," Bruce told Marlin. "I understand. Why trust a shark—right?"

Bruce studied the two smaller fish. "How would you morsels like to come to a little get-together I'm having?"

Dory smiled. "You mean like a party?"

"Yeah, right—a party. What do you say?" Bruce asked.

Dory looked over at Marlin and said, "Ooh, I love parties. That sounds like fun."

Marlin couldn't believe his ears. A shark party? He was sure they wanted to eat him.

"You know," said Marlin, "parties are fun, and it's tempting. But we can't because—"

Bruce wrapped a fin around each fish. They were trapped! "Aw, come on," he said. "I insist."

"Oookay," Marlin said nervously, "that's all that matters. . . . "

Bruce led Marlin and Dory over a rocky ridge into an undersea crater. The giant hole was littered with floating sea mines. Heavy iron chains moored them in place.

"Hey, look!" said Dory, pointing to the mines. "Balloons! It *is* a party!"

Bruce laughed. "Mind your distance, though. Those 'balloons' can be a bit dodgy. You wouldn't want one of them to pop!"

Bruce weaved safely through the mines, taking Dory and Marlin with him. They drew closer to a shipwreck—a sunken submarine. They peered inside through a hole blasted in its middle.

"Anchor! Chum!" Bruce called out. "We've got company!"

A hammerhead shark and a mako shark circled below. "Well, it's about time, mate," said Anchor, the hammerhead, anxiously.

Chum agreed. "We've already gone through the snacks. And I'm still starving."

Bruce pushed Marlin and Dory down into the sub. *More sharks!* Marlin thought. And they were all snapping their jaws hungrily.

Brrring! A diving bell rang.

"Right, then, the meeting has officially come to order," Bruce said, ushering them into the group. Then he swam to a rusted makeshift podium.

All the sharks turned to him, listening closely.

It is *a meeting!* Marlin thought.

"Let us all say the pledge," Bruce continued.

Together, all the sharks recited, "I am a nice shark. Not a mindless eating machine. If I am to change this image, I must first change myself. Fish are friends. Not food."

Bruce nodded. "Today's meeting is Step Five: Bring a Fish Friend. Now, do you all have your friends?"

"Got mine!" Anchor said proudly. He lifted a fin. A scared, shaking fish peeked out.

"Hey there!" Dory said, waving.

Meet
the
Characters!

Dory

Hi, I'm Dory! I'm a blue tang, and I love to swim. I suffer from short-term memory loss, so I sometimes need to be reminded of all the friends I've met. Let me introduce you to some of them. . . .

Nemo

Nemo is a clownfish and one of
my best friends. One of his fins is
smaller than the other, but that
doesn't stop him from being an
excellent swimmer.

Marlin

Marlin is Nemo's dad.
He's a clownfish, too.
He's a little overprotective,
but that's just because he
loves Nemo so much.

Nemo's Friends

Nemo has three good friends at school.

Pearl

Pearl is a pink flapjack octopus.

Tad

Tad is a yellow longnose butterfly fish.

Sheldon

Sheldon is a sea horse.

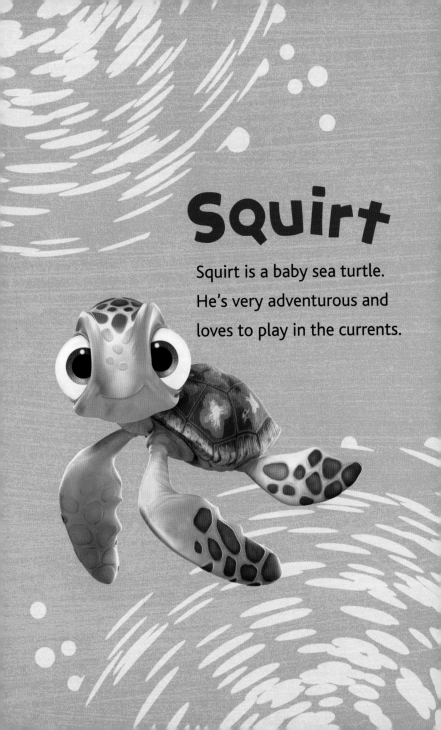

Squirt

Squirt is a baby sea turtle. He's very adventurous and loves to play in the currents.

Crush

Crush is Squirt's dad.
He's 150 years old!

Sharks!

Anchor

Anchor is a hammerhead shark.
See how his head looks like a big hammer?

Chum

Chum is a mako shark.

Bruce

Bruce is a great white shark and the leader of Fish-Eaters Anonymous.

The Tank Gang

The tank gang lives in a fish tank in a dentist's office in Sydney, Australia.

Gill

Gill is a moorish idol. He dreams of being free again.

Peach

Peach is a starfish. She loves to watch the dentist work on his patients.

Bloat

Bloat is a blowfish.
When he gets angry,
he **blows** up!

Bubbles

Bubbles is a yellow tang.
He loves the bubbles that
come out of the treasure
chest in the fish tank.

Gurgle

Gurgle is a royal gramma fish and a huge germophobe!

Jacques

Jacques is a cleaner shrimp. He helps keep the fish tank clean.

Deb
and
Flo

Deb is a black-and-white
humbug who thinks her
reflection is her twin sister, Flo.

Nigel

Nigel is a brown pelican.
He loves to hang out
at the window of the
dentist's office and gossip.

Character Studies

Here's a look at some of the early sketches and illustrations created by the Pixar artists as they developed each character.

Nemo

Marlin

Sheldon   Tad

Pearl

Dory

Sharks

Crush

Squirt

The Tank Gang

Bubbles

Gill

GILL
JAMES S. BAKER
MAR 30 2000

GILL

Bloat

Peach

Gurgle

Jacques

Deb and Flo

"How 'bout you, Chum?" Bruce asked.

"Oh, well . . . I, um . . . seem to have misplaced my . . . uh . . . friend," Chum said, embarrassed. He smiled just enough to reveal the skeletal remains of a fish tail stuck between his teeth.

"That's all right, Chum," said Bruce. "I had a feeling this would be a difficult step. You can help yourself to one of my friends."

"Aw, thanks, mate," Chum said, hugging Marlin tightly. "A little chum for Chum, eh?"

Marlin sighed nervously.

"I'll start the testimonies. It's been three weeks since my last fish, on my honor, or may I be chopped up and made into soup."

The other sharks clapped. "You're an inspiration to all of us!"

Bruce looked around. "Who's next?"

Dory swam up to the podium. Marlin groaned. What was she doing?

"Hi, I'm Dory. And, uh, well . . . I don't

think I've ever eaten a fish!" she said.

Everyone applauded. "Good on ya, mate," said one shark.

"That's incredible," said another.

While the sharks were distracted, Marlin freed himself. He tried to get Dory's attention at the podium.

Then Bruce spotted Marlin out of the corner of his eye. "How 'bout you, mate? What's your problem?" he asked.

Nervously, Marlin answered, "Me? I don't have a problem."

Bruce didn't believe Marlin and pushed him up to the podium. Excited to see that he was a clownfish, the sharks asked Marlin to tell them a joke.

"So the sea mollusk says to the sea cucumber . . ." Marlin was struggling to entertain the sharks when he spied a hole in the roof. And there, dangling from a piece of metal, was a diver's mask!

CHAPTER 5

It was the same mask that had dropped into the water when Nemo was taken away.

Maybe it would give Marlin a clue! A way to find his son.

"Nemo," Marlin said under his breath.

"Nemo," said Chum with a confused stare. "I don't get it."

"For a clownfish he's not that funny," Bruce agreed.

"No, no, no," Marlin said as he floated up toward the mask. "He's my son. He was taken by these divers."

"Bloody humans!" exclaimed Chum.

"They think they own everything."

"Now, there is a father. Lookin' for his little boy," Bruce said.

The shark sniffled, thinking of poor little Nemo separated from his dad. He wiped away a tear as Marlin and Dory swam closer to the mask. There were markings on it. Human writing.

"Ugh! What do these markings mean?" Marlin asked Dory. "I can't read human."

Dory grabbed the mask. "Well, then we gotta find a fish that can read this!" She dove down to the sharks.

"No, no, no!" Marlin yelled after Dory. This was their chance to escape. The sharks were all in a group hug, comforting Bruce.

Marlin reached for the mask.

"Hey! That's mine!" Dory shouted. "Give it back!"

Marlin pulled one side of the mask and Dory pulled the other in a tug-of-war. The mask snapped, hitting Dory's face.

"Ow!" Dory cried.

"Oh, I'm sorry," Marlin said quickly. "Are you okay? I'm so sorry!"

Dory rubbed her face. "Am I bleeding?"

"Dory?" asked Bruce. "Are you o—" He noticed some blood. "Oooooh!" He edged closer.

"Intervention!" yelled Anchor and Chum. Just as Bruce snapped his jaws shut, the other two sharks pulled him away. He missed Dory by an inch.

"Just a bite!" Bruce begged.

"Now, you hold it together, mate!" Anchor cried.

"Remember, Bruce," Chum said. "Fish are friends. Not food."

But Bruce wasn't listening. His mouth opened wider and wider. The smell of blood awoke his need to eat fish.

"Food!" he yelled, lunging again.

"Dory! Look out!" Marlin cried. He and Dory took hold of the mask together and awkwardly swam away.

"I'm having fish tonight!" Bruce shouted, diving after them.

Marlin and Dory swam faster and faster through the submarine. They had to escape the hungry shark!

"Look! Here's something!" Dory stopped in the torpedo room. She slowly read the letters written near a broken-down door. "*E-S-C-A-P-E*. I wonder what that means?" she asked herself out loud. "It's funny because it's spelled just like the word *escape*!"

Suddenly, the huge shark burst into the room. "Here's Brucie!"

Marlin and Dory raced through the door. Then Marlin stopped. "Wait a minute! You can read?"

"I can read?" Dory repeated, confused by the question. Then she remembered. "That's right! I can read!" she cried.

Marlin held the mask out to her. "W-well, then, here, read this. Now!"

Just then Bruce rammed his way out of the submarine. He chomped down, narrowly missing the two fish and catching the mask between his teeth.

"Aaah!" Marlin and Dory screamed. Bruce wrenched the mask from their fins.

The two fish raced away. *We need a place to hide,* thought Marlin. *But where?*

There! It was a torpedo tube at the side of the sub. Bruce could never fit inside.

Marlin led Dory into the tube. But their escape was blocked by a heavy torpedo.

Bruce slammed into the tube.

"Sorry about Bruce, mates!" Anchor and Chum called, swimming close by. "He's really a nice guy!"

Slam! Bruce charged again.

Marlin peered out. The diver's mask!

It was still dangling from Bruce's mouth! "I need to get that mask!" he shouted.

"Okay!" said Dory helpfully.

"No, no, noooo!" Marlin cried.

But Dory had already pushed a bolt, which released the torpedo. It slid out, pushing Marlin and Dory along with it—right into Bruce's mouth.

The shark snapped his teeth, ready for the tasty morsels. But the torpedo was in the way. His mouth couldn't close as he bit down on the hard metal.

Marlin and Dory grabbed the mask, then swam back inside the tube.

Furious, Bruce spat out the torpedo.

"Oh, no!" Anchor and Chum gasped. "Swim away! Swim away!"

The torpedo struck a floating mine. *Boom!* It exploded, setting off a chain reaction. Each explosion was bigger than the one before. *Boom! Boom! Boom!*

CHAPTER 6

Far, far away from his father, Nemo was plunged into unfamiliar water, where he landed on a plant of some kind. He peeked from behind the leafy fronds and called out, "Dad?"

There was no answer.

He gazed at all the new sights around him. Small, strange objects were everywhere: a miniature pirate ship, a tiny treasure chest, some sort of hut, a volcano with red lights flashing along the sides to look like lava, and finally, three giant tiki heads.

Terrified, Nemo tried to swim away. But

instead, he bumped into a transparent wall—then another, and another. He was in some sort of glass box!

Outside one glass wall, people sat in a waiting room. On the other side, a dentist approached a patient. Nemo heard them speaking, so he swam closer to the sound of their voices. The dentist, Dr. Sherman, saw Nemo and walked over to the tank. "Hello, little fellah," he said to Nemo. Then he turned to his patient and told him, "I found that guy struggling for life out on the reef and I saved him."

Nemo watched the dentist for a few more moments, then began to hear whispering behind him. Scared, he slowly backed away from the voices and bumped into the treasure chest. Hundreds of tiny bubbles poured out.

"Buuuuuubbbbbles!" cried a voice. A yellow tang fish charged at Nemo. Nemo dodged the fish. Then he watched the fish attempt to put the bubbles back in the chest.

"My bubbles!" cried Bubbles, the yellow tang, protectively.

Nemo raced into a nearby diver's helmet. But as soon as he was hidden, he saw a dark figure approaching. It got closer and closer until it was looking at Nemo up close.

"Bonjour," a tiny cleaner shrimp named Jacques said.

Nemo bolted out of the helmet and right into Bloat, a blowfish. "Whoa! Take it easy. Slow down, little fellah. There's nothing to worry about," Bloat said.

Nemo quickly looked around him and saw that he was surrounded by all kinds of fish. There were also a starfish named Peach, a black-and-white humbug named Deb, and a royal gamma named Gurgle.

"I wanna go home," Nemo said to his audience. "Do you know where my dad is?"

"Honey, your dad's probably back at the pet store," Peach said.

Nemo looked at the starfish curiously. "Pet store?" he asked.

All the fish chimed in at once. "Pet Palace," Gurgle said.

"Fish-O-Rama," added Deb.

"Mail order," said Bubbles.

Nemo still seemed a little confused. "I'm from the ocean," he timidly told the fish.

"The ocean?" Gurgle yelled.

The rest of the tank fish gasped.

"Wow. The big blue. What's it like?" asked Bubbles.

"Uh . . ." Nemo faltered. "Big . . . and blue."

"I knew it!" Bubbles exclaimed.

"Kid, if there's anything you need, just ask your auntie Deb. Or if I'm not around, you can always talk to my sister, Flo." Deb indicated her reflection in the glass. Nemo realized she thought it was her twin sister.

All of a sudden, Peach yelled out, "Root canal!"

The Tank Gang raced toward Peach to see the dental procedure that was in progress. They all watched with great interest, commenting as the dentist worked.

Just then, a pelican flew into the open window by the fish tank. "What did I miss?" the bird asked. "Am I late?"

"Hey, Nigel," Peach said to the pelican. "Root canal, and it's a doozy."

Nigel looked over at the tank and noticed the new little fish. "Hello. Who's this?" he asked.

"New guy," Deb said.

As Nigel leaned closer to the tank to give Nemo a proper hello, Dr. Sherman walked into the room. "Hey!" he yelled. "No, no, no! Those aren't your fish. Those are mine. Shoo!"

Nigel let out a loud squawk and flew away. As he took off, he knocked over some of Dr. Sherman's things.

The dentist leaned down and picked up a picture in a frame that had fallen to the floor and cracked. "Hey, little fellah," he said to Nemo. "Say hello to your new mummy. She's gonna be here Friday to pick you up! You're her present. . . ."

As soon as Dr. Sherman walked away, the Tank Gang began to mutter, "Oh. Darla . . . not her . . . she's bad news."

"What?" Nemo asked. "What's wrong with her?"

"Poor Chuckles," Deb said.

"He was her present last year," said Bloat.

"She's a fish killer," Peach added.

Nemo was horrified. "I can't go with that girl," the little clownfish said. "I have to get back to my dad."

Getting more worried by the second,

Nemo began to swim wildly around the tank. He ended up stuck in the filter tube. "Help me!" he cried.

"Oh, no!" the Tank Gang yelled. "We gotta get him outta there."

They all rushed over to Nemo but stopped short when they heard someone say, "Nobody touch him."

They looked behind them and saw Gill, a moorish idol fish, come out of the shadows.

"Can you help me?" Nemo asked him, struggling.

"No. You got yourself in there, you can get yourself out," Gill replied. He started to swim away, but decided to give the little fish a bit of helpful advice. "Alternate wiggling your fins and tail."

"I—I can't. I have a bad fin," Nemo said.

"Never stopped *me*," Gill said, showing Nemo his own severed pectoral fin. "Just think about what you need to do."

Nemo tried and tried, and with one last push, he freed himself.

The Tank Gang burst into cheers. "Pretty good, kid. You did it!" they cried.

Gill didn't join in the celebration. He was in a corner, deep in thought.

Peach looked over at him and said, "Uh-oh. I've seen that look before. What are you thinking about?"

"I'm thinkin' . . . tonight we give the kid a proper reception," Gill said.

CHAPTER 7

The next morning, Marlin opened his eyes—only to find Dory snoring loudly by his side. As he looked around, Marlin realized that they were hanging on top of the submarine by a strap, over a huge pit. And they were sleeping on the diver's mask.

The mask! They still had it!

Marlin peered down. The pit seemed bottomless.

"Dory, wake up," Marlin said, shaking her gently.

Dory mumbled something about a bad haircut but continued to sleep.

Marlin was getting frustrated. "Get up!" he said forcefully.

"Aagh!" Dory screamed and jumped, waking up.

At that moment, the submarine began to slide off the cliff. Dory and Marlin raced away from it just in time. They barely missed being crushed by the falling sub.

Marlin looked around frantically. "The mask," he said. "Where's the mask?"

Dory and Marlin both looked down and saw the mask disappear into the blackness of the deep water.

"No! No! Get it! Get the mask!" Marlin yelled. He swam after it, followed by Dory.

Blackness swallowed the two fish up. They couldn't even see their own fins.

Marlin swam up to the lighter-colored water, panting with fear.

"It just keeps going on, doesn't it?" Dory said.

She swam a little deeper, then popped back up next to Marlin. She looked surprised to see him. "Hey! What are you doing?"

"It's gone. I've lost the mask," Marlin said.

"What, did you drop it?" asked Dory innocently.

"You dropped it!" Marlin cried. "That was my only chance of finding my son. And now it's gone."

"Hey, Mr. Grumpy Gills," Dory sang out. "When life gets you down, you know what you gotta do?"

"I don't want to know what you gotta do," Marlin said crossly.

"Just keep swimming," Dory told him. "What do we do? We swim, swim."

Slowly, he swam down with Dory. Farther . . . farther . . . farther . . . into the deep.

"Dory," he said after a while. "Do you see anything?"

Dory gasped, unable to see in the total darkness. "Who's that?"

"Who could it be? It's me!" Marlin replied.

"Are you my conscience?" asked Dory.

"Yeah, yeah, yeah. I'm your conscience. Now, I want you to tell me—do you see anything?" Marlin asked.

"I see a light! Over there!" Dory exclaimed.

"I see it, too!" Marlin cried.

A small glowing ball of light floated in the distance. Marlin couldn't look away. It had him under some kind of spell. It made him feel happy.

It apparently had the same effect on Dory. "It's so pretty. I want to touch it," she said.

The light danced in the water.

Dory and Marlin followed the light.

Marlin thought it was strange that the light made him feel happy. But then he had a funny feeling. Like something was watching him. He turned around. A deadly anglerfish with huge fangs floated right behind them! The light dangled from its antenna, like bait.

"Good feeling's gone," he said to Dory.

Marlin and Dory raced into the darkness. The anglerfish chased them. Its glowing orb gave them their only light.

"I can't see! I don't know where I'm going!" Marlin cried.

Suddenly, the light fell on something familiar. The diver's mask! But the anglerfish was gaining on them—its jaws ready to snap!

Marlin pulled Dory down deeper. The anglerfish shot past, missing them in the darkness.

But they were safe only for a moment. The anglerfish came back, searching for them. It swung close to Marlin, lighting the water nearby.

"Hey, look, a mask!" Dory exclaimed.

"Read it!" Marlin said as he launched himself forward in the water, leading the anglerfish away.

"Uh . . . I'm sorry, but if you could just bring him a little closer?" Dory asked. "I kinda need the light."

Marlin swam all around Dory with the anglerfish right on his tail. He ducked between two rocks, safe for a second. He grabbed the antenna light and directed it toward Dory.

"The first line is 'P. Sherman,'" Dory said. "Second line . . . '42 Waaa—'"

Marlin was yanked up and away from the rocks. The anglerfish swallowed him and its own antenna whole.

In the sudden darkness, Dory said, "Light, please."

Inside the anglerfish, Marlin screamed. The anglerfish opened its mouth and Marlin shot out—along with the light.

"The second line is '42 Wallaby Way,'" Dory said.

"That's great," Marlin said anxiously. "Just finish up here. Speed-read."

As the furious anglerfish barreled straight toward them, Dory shouted out, "'Sydney'! It's 'Sydney'!"

"Duck!" Marlin cried.

Dory dove as Marlin lifted the mask.

The anglerfish crashed into the mask, sending them into a spin.

Then all was quiet. Marlin squinted. He thought for sure he had been eaten. The anglerfish was now wedged between the mask and a rock. It flapped around helplessly, stuck.

"Ha, ha!" Marlin laughed as he and Dory swam toward the surface.

"No eating here tonight!" the two fish sang together.

Then Marlin turned to Dory. "So what did the mask say?"

" 'P. Sherman. 42 Wallaby Way, Sydney.' " She gasped, not believing it herself. "I remembered what it said! I usually forget things, but I remembered it that time. P. Sherman, 42—"

"Wait!" Marlin interrupted. "Now, where is that?"

"I don't know," Dory replied. "But who cares? I remembered!"

CHAPTER 8

The dentist's office was closed for the night. The tank was dark, and Nemo slept soundly in the tiki hut.

Jacques approached Nemo quietly and said, "Psst. Nemo."

Nemo didn't stir, so Jacques threw a small pebble at him. Still no response from Nemo. Jacques threw another pebble at him, but the little fish slept on. In frustration, Jacques threw a whole bunch of pebbles.

Nemo woke with a start.

"Follow me," Jacques told the new fish.

He led Nemo to the center of the tank,

which was lit up by the red gleam of the fake lava flow.

Nemo heard a strange low chanting, then saw something moving behind the tiki heads. Bubbles, Gurgle, then Bloat surfaced from behind the heads.

Jacques and Nemo began the long climb up the face of the volcano. As he passed by Deb and Peach, Nemo was given a ceremonial whack with the kelp fronds they held.

Then, at the peak of the volcano, Nemo saw Gill floating silently.

"State your name," Gill told Nemo.

"N-N-Nemo," the scared fish stammered.

"Brother Bloat, proceed," said Gill.

"Nemo. Newcomer of orange and white," Bloat said solemnly. "You have been called forth to the summit of Mount Wannahockaloogie to join with us in the fraternal bonds of tankhood."

Nemo had no idea what Bloat was saying. "Huh?" he asked.

"We want you in our club, kid," Peach said.

"If you are able to swim through . . . *the Ring of Fire!*" Bloat said dramatically.

Nemo looked around, confused.

Bloat gave Jacques a stern look and whispered to him, "Turn on the Ring of Fire."

At that moment, a wall of bubbles rose out of the volcano.

Gill motioned to Nemo to swim through the bubbles to him.

Nemo took a deep breath and closed his eyes. He hesitated, then swam with all his might. He swam through the Ring of Fire, bumping right into Gill.

Gill gave Nemo a big smile and lifted him high over his head. "From this moment on, you will now be known as Shark Bait," he said.

"Okay," Gill added to the rest of the Tank

Gang. "Shark Bait's one of us now, agreed?"

The whole tank agreed.

"And we can't send him off to his death. Darla's coming in five days," Gill said. "So we're gonna get him *outta* here. We're gonna help him escape."

"Escape?" Nemo squeaked. "Really?"

"We're *all* gonna escape," Gill said.

All the fish laughed. "Not another one of your escape plans," Gurgle said.

"Sorry, but they just never work," Deb added.

"Yeah, why should this be any different?" Bloat asked.

Gill turned serious and pointed to Nemo. "'Cause we've got him."

Nemo gulped. "Me?" he asked.

Gill put his fin around Nemo. "You see that filter? You're the only one small enough to get in and out of that thing," Gill said.

Nemo started to feel the pressure.

"What we need you to do," Gill said, "is take a pebble inside there and jam the gears. You do that, and this tank's gonna get filthier and filthier by the minute. Pretty soon the dentist'll have to clean the tank himself—and when he does, he'll take us out of the tank, put us in individual bags; then we'll roll ourselves down the counter, out of the window, off the awning, into the bushes, across the street, and into the harbor.

"Who's with me?" Gill asked, turning to the rest of the Tank Gang.

Everyone raised a fin in agreement, except Gurgle. "I think you're nuts! No offense, kid, but you're not the best swimmer," he said.

"He's fine. He can do this!" Gill said. "So, Shark Bait, what do you think?"

Nemo looked around at all the friends he'd made and thought about seeing his father again. "Let's do it," he said with a smile.

CHAPTER 9

Marlin had the address from the mask: 42 Wallaby Way, Sydney. But where was Wallaby Way? Where was Sydney?

He had to ask for directions.

A school of silvery moonfish swirled past. Maybe they knew.

"Excuse me," Marlin said as they rushed by. "Uh—hello?"

The moonfish darted this way and that, constantly moving.

"Hey! Hold it!" Marlin shouted. "Wait a minute! I'm trying to talk to you."

Again, they hurried by.

"One quick question!" Marlin pleaded. "Please? And they're gone again!"

Just then, Dory swam closer by. "P. Sherman, 42 Wallaby Way," she recited. She'd been repeating the address ever since she'd remembered it. "42 Wallaby Way."

It was driving Marlin crazy.

"Okay. All right, here's the thing," he told her. "I think it's best if I just carry on from here . . . by myself."

Dory paused, not understanding. "Huh?"

This was so hard to say. Marlin tried again. "I don't want to hurt your feelings."

"You want me to leave?" Dory asked in disbelief.

"Well, I mean not . . . Yes. It's just, you know . . . I can't afford any more delays, and you're one of those fish that cause delays."

Dory's eyes opened wide. "You mean . . . you don't like me?"

"No! Of course I like you," Marlin

explained. "Oh! Don't cry. I like you—"

All of a sudden, a group of moonfish stopped in front of them. "Hey, you!" one said to Marlin.

They all hovered there, staring at Marlin.

"Lady," said the fish. "Is this guy bothering you?"

"Um, I don't remember." Dory sniffled. Then she turned to Marlin. "Were you?"

"Hey!" Marlin said suddenly. He finally had their attention! "Do you guys know how I can get to P. Sherman—"

"Look, pal, we're talking to the lady, not you." The fish smiled at Dory, trying to cheer her up. "You like impressions? Okay," the fish said to the others. "Just like in rehearsal, gentlemen . . ."

The moonfish swam into different positions, forming the shape of a swordfish.

"So what are we? Take a guess?" they asked.

Marlin takes Nemo to his very first day of school.

Nemo meets his new classmates
Sheldon, Pearl, and Tad.

Uh-oh! There's a scuba diver behind Nemo.

Marlin asks a regal blue tang fish named
Dory for help finding his son.

Bruce, Chum, and Anchor may be sharks,
but they think fish are friends, not food.

Marlin and Dory run into a hungry anglerfish!

"*Bonjour!*" Jacques and the other members
of the tank gang welcome Nemo to the fish tank.

Gill, the leader of the tank gang,
hatches an escape plan.

Dory and Marlin ask the moonfish for directions
to 42 Wallaby Way in Sydney, Australia.

The two friends stumble into a
forest of stinging jellyfish!

"Hey, dude!" Crush and the other sea turtles point
Marlin and Dory toward Sydney.

A giant whale carries Marlin and Dory
the rest of the way to Sydney.

Home at last!

Dory perked up. "Oh, I've seen one of those," she said.

"I'm a fish with a nose like a *sword*," one of the moonfish said, giving her a hint.

"Wait . . . wait . . . um . . ." Dory said.

"It's a swordfish!" Marlin put in.

"Hey, Clown Boy. Let the lady guess," another fish scolded Marlin.

The moonfish did more impressions. They changed into a lobster, an octopus, a ship . . . But Dory didn't get a single one right.

"Would *somebody* please give me directions?" Marlin shouted angrily.

The moonfish switched places again. This time they looked like a clownfish. An angry clownfish—just like Marlin.

Finally, Dory laughed.

This is useless, Marlin thought. He swam off.

"Hey! Come back!" Dory followed him. "What's the matter?"

Marlin turned to her. "What's the matter? While they're doing their silly little impressions, I am miles from home, with a fish that can't even remember her own name." He sighed. "Meanwhile, my son is out there. . . . But it doesn't matter, 'cause no fish in this entire ocean is gonna help me."

"Well, I'm helping you," Dory told him. "Wait right here."

She hurried back to the school of fish. "Guys, any of you heard of P. Sherman, 42 Wallaby Way, Sydney?" she asked politely.

"Sydney? Oh, sure," said one of the fish.

"You wouldn't know how to get there, would you?" asked Dory.

"What you wanna do is follow the EAC. That's, uh, East Australian Current," the fish explained.

The moonfish shifted places so that they looked like wavy lines in the water: the East

Australian Current. "Big current—can't miss it."

Then they turned into an arrow. "It's in that direction. And then you're gonna follow that for about, uh, three leagues, and that little baby's gonna float you right past Sydney."

"Great!" Marlin swam over. "That's great! Dory, you did it!"

"Oh, please. I'm just your little helper—helpin' along," Dory said cheerfully.

"Well, listen, fellahs, thank you," Marlin called to the moonfish.

"Don't mention it. Just loosen up. Okay, buddy?" they replied.

"Bye," Dory said as she and Marlin swam off.

"Oh, hey, ma'am?" said the fish. "One more thing."

Dory turned and swam back to the moonfish. "Yes?"

"When you come to this trench?" The fish formed a picture of a long, narrow ditch with very steep sides. "Swim through it. Not over it!"

"Trench," Dory repeated. "Through it. Not over it. I'll remember!"

Then she turned to catch up with Marlin, who was already on his way.

CHAPTER 10

A little while later, Marlin was swimming along the ocean floor. Dory trailed close behind.

All at once, Marlin stopped short. They were at the edge of a long, dark, spooky-looking trench.

"Okay, let's go!" Dory cried.

"Bad trench. Come on," he told Dory. "We're gonna swim over this thing."

Dory shook her head. "Whoa, partner. Little red flag goin' up. Something's telling me we should swim through it, not over it."

Marlin's jaw dropped. "Are you even

looking at this thing? It's got death written all over it!"

"I'm sorry. But I really, really, really think we should swim through. Come on, trust me on this."

"Trust you?" Marlin asked.

"Yes. Trust. It's what friends do," Dory said.

"Look!" Marlin said, trying to distract Dory. "Something shiny."

"Where?" said Dory.

"Oh, it just swam over the trench. Come on, we'll follow it," Marlin said.

"Okay!" Dory happily agreed, forgetting about the moonfish's warning.

The two fish swam over the trench to clear blue water. In the distance they could see the fast-moving East Australian Current.

"We should be there in no time," said Marlin.

Dory wasn't listening. She was staring at a tiny jellyfish floating just in front of her. She moved closer. "Hey, little guy."

"You wanted to go through the trench," Marlin said with a laugh.

Dory reached for the jellyfish. "I shall call him Squishy. And he shall be *my* Squishy. Come here, little Squishy!"

But as Dory tried to touch the jellyfish, it stung her. "Ow!" she shouted.

"Dory!" Marlin gasped. "That's a jellyfish!"

"Bad Squishy!" Dory said as Marlin pushed the jellyfish away from her.

"Shoo! Get away!" he said. Then he turned to Dory.

"Come here. Let me see that." Marlin held Dory's fin to examine the sting. Neither of them noticed more and more jellyfish swimming closer. The jellyfish were floating down from above.

"Hey, how come it didn't sting you?" Dory asked.

"It did," Marlin answered. "It's just that I live in this anemone and I'm used to these kinds of stings. It doesn't look too bad," he told Dory. "You're gonna be fine. But now we know, don't we, that we don't want to touch these again. Let's be thankful this time it was just a little one."

As they turned to go, hundreds of jellyfish blocked their path. Marlin couldn't believe his eyes. This was seriously dangerous.

"Don't move!" he ordered.

More and more jellyfish were coming. There were jellyfish as far as he could see!

"This is bad, Dory." Marlin looked around. Dory was bouncing on top of a large jellyfish like it was a trampoline.

"Hey, watch this! Boing! Boing!" She

laughed. "You can't catch me," she called to Marlin.

Oh, no, Marlin thought. *She thinks this is fun.*

He reached for her, but she bounced onto another jellyfish. Marlin closed his eyes, not wanting to see his friend get hurt again. But Dory didn't scream. Marlin opened his eyes and saw her happily bouncing along. Then he remembered that the tops of jellyfish don't sting.

"All right, listen to me!" he said to Dory. "I have an idea—a game."

"I love games!" Dory cried.

"All right. Here's the game: whoever can hop the fastest out of these jellyfish wins," Marlin said.

"Okay! Okay!" Dory exclaimed.

"Rules, rules, rules! You can't touch the tentacles. Only the tops," Marlin ordered.

"Something about tentacles. Got it," Dory

said. "On your mark. Get set. Go!"

Dory took off jumping. Marlin followed slowly behind. "Now, be careful," he told himself.

"Wheeeeee!" Dory giggled, leaping from one jellyfish to the next.

Marlin moved faster, trying to keep up. *Boing!* This was . . . kind of fun! He was actually having a good time!

"Dory, are you hungry?" asked Marlin.

"Huh? Hungry?" Dory said.

"Yeah, 'cause you're about to eat my bubbles!" Marlin cried.

Then he bounded out of the jellyfish forest, feeling the pull of the East Australian Current nearby. "The clownfish is the winner!" he shouted to Dory. "We did it!"

But Dory wasn't there.

"Oh, no!" Marlin groaned. He darted back to find her.

"Dory?" he called, peering through the

jellyfish. Then he spotted her—wrapped up tight in a jellyfish's tentacles.

Without even thinking, Marlin pushed through the other jellyfish. He shot straight through the giant tentacles and grabbed Dory.

Marlin was a fish on a mission—to save Dory. "Am I disqualified?" she asked, barely able to speak.

"You're actually winning. But you've got to stay awake!" Marlin said.

Marlin held Dory with one fin. He paddled with the other. The water was thick with jellyfish. He could see one small patch of blue ahead. He had to reach it!

Barreling through the jellyfish, he shielded Dory with his body. As he went, he was stung again and again. With each new sting, he slowed down. He grew weaker. "Stay awake!" he kept saying—to Dory and to himself.

"Stay . . ." With his last bit of strength, Marlin pushed past a gigantic jellyfish. ". . . awake."

He floated into the safety of the clear open water.

Weary, he saw something up ahead. Something big and green and moving very slowly . . . and then everything went black.

CHAPTER 11

Back in the fish tank, Nemo had been swimming every day with Gill, learning how to use his small injured fin. Already he was swimming faster, more smoothly.

Nemo knew he didn't have much time. Only two more days. Then Darla would come to take him away.

As Nemo swam past, Gill noticed Nemo's eyes on his withered fin.

"My first escape," said Gill grimly. "Landed on dental tools. I was aiming for the toilet."

"The toilet?" Nemo asked.

"All drains lead to the ocean, kid," Gill replied.

Nemo thought for a minute and then looked at Gill seriously. He knew he had to do everything he could to help them all escape.

It was finally time for the next step in the plan: jamming the filter so that the tank would get dirty.

The fish gathered by the bubbling filter.

"Now, once you get in, you swim down to the bottom of the chamber, and I'll talk you through the rest," Gill said to Nemo. It was up to the little fish to stop the machine.

Nemo held his breath and popped his head through the surface. He saw the water wheel.

Then he leaped into the air and onto the

wheel. He flapped as the wheel spun, then flipped himself through the gap. He landed in the bottom well of the filter. He was inside!

Gill was right outside the filter. He scooped up a pebble from the bottom of the tank and threw it to Nemo.

"Do you see a small opening?" Gill asked.

Nemo nodded.

"Inside it, you'll see a rotating rod. Wedge that pebble up against the rod to stop it turning. Careful, Shark Bait."

Nemo followed Gill's instructions. After one failed attempt, the whirring noise stopped. The filter was jammed!

"That's great, kid," Gill said. "Now go up the tube and out."

Nemo grinned. He began to swim out of the filter. But the pebble slipped out of place. *Whirrrr!* The filter started working again!

The giant blade jerked, then turned. It was pulling Nemo back into the filter. In seconds he'd be sucked inside, toward the rotating blade.

"Gill! Help me!" cried Nemo.

Gill raced over to a plastic plant. "Stay calm, kid. Just don't panic."

Together, the Tank Gang yanked on the plant. They managed to pull off a branch and shove it into the filter tube.

"Grab hold of this!" Gill called to Nemo.

Nemo stretched his fin. Closer, closer . . .

He had it! But he was still about to fall into the sharp, spinning blade!

Gill and the others held on to the branch and pulled—hard.

Nemo was suddenly free. He was outside the filter—safe, but shaken up pretty badly. The little fish began to cry.

"Gill, don't make him go back in there," Peach said.

"No. We're done," Gill said, unable to look any of the other fish in the eye.

CHAPTER 12

Back in the ocean, Marlin rubbed his head. He felt a little funny, like he'd been sleeping too long. Then he remembered the jellyfish. He *had* been sleeping—recovering from the poisonous jellyfish stings.

He blinked, trying to focus. Two giant eyes stared back at him—and he was moving! He was riding on the back of a sea turtle! Marlin gazed around. Hundreds of sea turtles were swimming all around him!

"Dude!" said the sea turtle. "We saw the whole thing. You got some serious thrill issues, dude. Awesome."

"Uh, so, Mr. Turtle?" Marlin said.

"Whoa, dude. Mr. Turtle is my father. Name is Crush."

"Crush? Really," Marlin said. "Listen, I need to get to the East Australian Current."

"You're riding on it," Crush told him. "Check it out."

Now that Marlin was looking around, he noticed that the sea turtles were surfing an endless ribbon of green sea. They weaved through the ocean, riding the current.

Suddenly the current dipped, then rose. Marlin gripped Crush's shell tightly.

"So what brings you on this fine day to the EAC?" asked Crush.

"Well, Dory and I need to go to Sydney— Dory. Is she all right?"

Crush pointed below, to another line of swimming turtles. Marlin spied a blue speck lying on one turtle's back. Dory!

Marlin jumped off Crush's back and dove

closer. He gasped. Dory was still.

"Oh, Dory!" he cried, burying his head in his fins. "I'm so sorry. This is all my fault."

All at once, Dory jumped up. "Twenty-nine . . . thirty!" she shouted. "Ready or not, here I come!"

She swam off, peeking under the shells of some small turtles. Young turtles popped out their heads and giggled.

"Catch me if you can!" Dory called, racing away.

Marlin sighed. Dory was fine.

The turtle kids formed a chain. They whipped around, and the last in line hurtled off the current.

"Oh, my goodness—" Marlin cried. He rushed to help.

But Crush appeared at his side and held him back.

"Kill the motor, dude. Let's see what Crush junior does flying solo."

That turtle was his son? But Crush was so calm!

"They find their way back," Crush explained.

"B-But, dude, how do you know when they're ready?" Marlin asked.

"You never really know. But when they know, you'll know," Crush said.

The little turtle paddled back into the current, giggling. "That was so cool!"

Then Crush turned to Marlin. "Intro. Jellyman, Offspring. Offspring, Jellyman."

Dory and all the other kids spotted Marlin. "Go on!" Dory nudged them. "Jump on him!"

The kids tumbled close to Marlin. "Did you really cross the Jellyfish Forest?" one asked.

"Did they sting you?" asked another.

"Where are you going?" asked a third.

"Well, you see, my son was taken away

from me." Marlin explained about Nemo and his search. The divers . . . the anglerfish . . . the sharks . . .

The young turtles listened to his story, fascinated. Then they swam off and told other turtles. A lobster overheard the story. She told another lobster while a dolphin dove nearby, listening, too.

That dolphin told another dolphin as they swam alongside a boat. A bird sat on the prow and heard the story, too. He told another bird while flying past Sydney Harbor—right near a flock of pelicans, which included Nigel.

"Nemo!" Nigel exclaimed as soon as he heard the story of the brave clownfish. He took off, heading for the dentist's office.

CHAPTER 13

Nigel landed in a flurry of feathers on the dentist's windowsill. "Where's Nemo?" he shouted.

Nemo swam to the side of the tank that faced the window. "What is it?" he asked.

"Your dad's been fightin' the entire ocean lookin' for you," Nigel said, and told Nemo about his father's adventures. The other fish in the tank gathered around. They wanted to hear the fantastic story Nigel was telling.

Nemo couldn't believe it! His dad hardly ever left the anemone.

"Shark Bait! Your dad is Superfish!" cried Bubbles.

All the tank fish cheered. Then they turned to Nemo, but he wasn't there.

"Shark Bait?" called Gill. Suddenly he spied the little fish. He was inside the filter!

Nemo gripped a pebble in his fin. It was a bigger one than last time, and he was determined to do it right. This time he would jam the filter!

After all, his dad was Superfish. And if his dad could be a Superfish, then Nemo was going to be one, too!

He struggled for a moment; then—

The pebble was in. *Whirrrrrrr!* The fan slowed, then stopped. All was quiet.

"You did it!" the tank fish cried as Nemo floated beside them.

"All right, gang," Gill said. "We have less than forty-eight hours before Darla gets here. This tank will get plenty dirty in that time, but we have to help it along any way we can. Be as gross as possible. We're gonna make this tank so filthy the dentist'll have to clean it."

Meanwhile, Marlin and Dory were saying good-bye to Crush and the other turtles.

"Get ready!" Crush told them. He twisted his head to look at the two fish riding on his back. "Your exit's coming up."

Marlin squinted. "Where?"

Dory pointed up ahead. "I see it! Right there!"

Marlin gulped. "You mean that swirling vortex of terror?"

"That's it, dude," Crush said.

The eddy swirled around and around a little past the current. "Okay, Jellyman. Go!" cried Crush. He swerved, and Marlin and

Dory tumbled from his shell, into the eddy.

They slid down the giant slide formed by the whirling current. Not far off, they could see Crush and the others still riding the EAC.

"Hey, look!" Dory cried. "Turtles!"

"Swim straight on through Sydney!" Crush directed them as they slid. "You tell your little dude I said hi."

Wait! Marlin remembered Nemo's question about the sea turtles.

"Crush! How old are you?" he shouted.

"A hundred and fifty, dude! And still young! Rock on!" Crush called as the current swept him off.

Marlin and Dory turned away. Now they faced dark, murky water. "We going in there?" Dory asked.

Marlin nodded. For the first time in a long while, he didn't feel nervous in the least. "We're gonna just swim straight," he said.

CHAPTER 14

Hours passed. Marlin and Dory swam and swam. The water was still dim and cloudy. Nothing seemed to have changed. They felt like they'd been swimming forever.

"Wait! I've definitely seen this floating speck before," Marlin said suddenly, pointing to something in the water. "That means we're going in circles, and that means we're not going straight! We gotta get to the surface. Follow me!"

"Whooaa!" said Dory. "Relax. Let's ask somebody for directions."

Marlin snorted. "Fine. Who do you want

to ask? The speck? There's nobody here!"

"Well, there has to be someone. It's the ocean, silly! We're not the only two in here," Dory said.

She gazed into the darkness. The water was so foggy, she couldn't see much farther than her nose.

Just then, a small shadow passed ahead of them.

"We don't know that fish!" Marlin said. "If we ask it for directions, it could ingest us and spit out our bones!"

"Come on," Dory said. "Trust me on this."

Marlin gazed at her jellyfish stings—the wounds she'd gotten because he didn't trust her before.

"All right," he said.

Dory smiled. "Excuse me! Little fellah?" she called out. "His son, Bingo—"

"Nemo," Marlin interrupted a little shakily. As the small shape moved closer, it didn't seem so small anymore.

"Nemo was taken to Sydney," Dory continued, "and it's really, really important we get there as fast as we can. So, can you help us out? Come on, little fellah."

"Dory, *I'm* a little fellah," Marlin said. "I don't think *that's* a little fellah."

Suddenly, the creature broke through a thick layer of murk. It was a giant blue whale!

The whale steamed toward them silently.

"Oh, big fellah! Maybe he only speaks whale." Dory tried again to explain their situation to the creature, this time talking whale. *"Neeeeeeemmmooouu-uuuuewasssszzzzzztii-iiiaaaakkkkeeennnnn..."*

"What are you doing?" Marlin asked nervously. "Are you sure you speak whale?"

He peered at the humongous creature. "He's swimming away. It's just as well. He might be hungry."

"Don't worry. Whales don't eat clownfish," Dory said calmly. "They eat krill."

Just then a hundred tiny shrimp rushed past, trying to escape the whale.

"Oh, look! Krill!" said Dory.

The whale opened its enormous mouth. Water flowed in, taking everything with it.

Marlin grabbed Dory. They turned tail and swam. But it was no use. The current was too strong. Marlin and Dory were swallowed up into the whale's vast mouth. It was big— very big. And very dark. And it looked like there was no way out.

CHAPTER 15

Meanwhile, the Tank Gang were busy in the dentist's office, admiring their dirty work.

"Would you look at that? Filthy. Absolutely filthy," Gill said. "And it's all thanks to you, kid. You made it possible."

The gang watched closely when Dr. Sherman walked into the office. He strode across the room to the tank, and stuck his hand inside the murky water. "Crikey! What a state!" he cried. "I better clean the fish tank before Darla gets here."

The Tank Gang cheered. Tomorrow was the day. Tomorrow they would all escape.

"Are you ready to see your dad, kid?" Gill asked Nemo.

Nemo nodded.

"You know," Gill added. "I wouldn't be surprised if he's out there in the harbor waiting for you right now."

Inside the whale's mouth, Marlin and Dory heard creaks and moans that echoed all around. Marlin wasn't going to swim around being trapped. He had to get out! He started by throwing himself forward.

Boom! He crashed against the curtain-like baleen that hung from the whale's jaw. But it didn't budge. Marlin rammed the baleen again and again. But it was no use.

Waves rose and fell inside the whale's mouth. Dory rode a swell, laughing like it was a ride.

Got your **swim fins?**

"We're in a whale!" Marlin shouted, starting to get angry. "Don't you get it?"

Dory looked surprised. "A whale?"

"A whale! 'Cause *you* had to ask for help. And now we're stuck here! I have to get out!" Marlin pounded the baleen. "I have to find my son. I have to tell him how old sea turtles are!"

Exhausted, Marlin dropped onto the whale's tongue. Suddenly, the whale lurched to a stop.

"What's going on?" asked Marlin.

"Don't know," Dory replied. "I'll ask him."

Dory made some more strange sounds.

The whale answered with a roar. "I think he says we've stopped," Dory offered.

"Well, of course we've stopped," Marlin said, annoyed.

Just then the water began to sink lower and lower. It was draining down the whale's throat. Any minute now, Marlin and Dory, too, would be forced down into the stomach.

The whale moaned. "He says it's time to let go!" Dory cried.

Marlin peered down the long, dark throat.

"Everything's gonna be all right," Dory said calmly.

"How do you know?" Marlin asked. "How do you know something bad isn't going to happen?"

"I don't!" Dory replied.

What else could he do? Marlin took a deep breath, then let go. The two fish tumbled down . . . down . . . down.

Suddenly, they were swept up in a gush of water.

In Sydney Harbor, the whale surfaced. Marlin and Dory shot out its spout in a jet of water. They tumbled through the air in a spray of mist and foam.

Splash! They hit the harbor water.

"We're alive!" Marlin cried.

"Look!" Dory pointed to a boat with writing on its side. "It says 'Sydney'!"

"You were right, Dory!" Marlin exclaimed. "We made it. We're gonna find my son!"

Marlin thanked the whale, then turned to Dory. "Okay, all we have to do is find the boat that took him," he said.

"Right," Dory agreed.

Marlin surfaced and gazed at the boats. There were hundreds of them, as far as he could see.

But he'd made it this far. And nothing would stop him from finding Nemo.

Marlin threw back his fins. "Come on, Dory. We can do this!"

CHAPTER 16

"It's morning, everyone!" Peach was stretching her arms, the first one awake in the tank. "Today's the day. The sun is shining, the tank is clean, and we are getting out of—"

Suddenly she gasped. The tank was clean?

Moments later, everyone gathered at the filter. They stared up in horror. It was a new filter—a huge, towering one. And it didn't have any moving parts they could break—or put a pebble into!

"Boss must have installed it last night while we were sleeping," Gill said, shaking his head, disappointed.

"The Aqua Scum 2003 is an all-purpose, self-cleaning, maintenance-free saltwater purifier." Peach was reading a booklet that lay open on the counter.

A red laser beam shot out from the filter, sweeping the water. "Temperature eighty-two degrees," an automated voice recited. "Ph balance normal."

The Tank Gang looked on in amazement. Then they realized what had happened. "Curse you, Aqua Scum!" cried Gurgle.

"That's it for the escape plan!" Bloat cried, inflating in anger. "It's ruined!"

"What are we going to do about . . ." Nemo panicked. The door of the dentist's office swung open.

"Darla!" shouted the Tank Gang.

"Stay down, kid," Gill said sharply.

A little boy walked into the waiting room with his mother. "False alarm," Bloat said.

Nemo sighed with relief. But then, before

he could move, he felt a net fall around him—a fishnet!

He was lifted up, up, up.

"Gill! Help me!" he shouted.

"Nemo!" Gill shouted back.

Quickly taking action, Gill swam as fast as he could over to Nemo and jumped into the net with him. With all his might, he started to swim down, in an attempt to get the net away from the dentist.

"C'mon, kid," Gill said to Nemo. "Swim down! Swim down!"

The rest of the Tank Gang jumped into the net as well, and they all swam down as hard as they could.

Just when Nemo thought he'd gotten free from the net, Dr. Sherman trapped him inside a plastic bag filled with water.

The dentist plopped Nemo on a counter and walked away.

The Tank Gang raced to that side of the

glass. "Roll, kid!" everyone told him. "Just roll! Keep going. You can do it."

Nemo twisted around and around. It was working. Slowly, the bag was moving.

The window! He saw it on the other side of the counter. If he could make it there, it would be one jump to the harbor below.

Then Dr. Sherman grabbed the bag. "Now that would be a nasty fall," he said, placing the bag on a tray.

Suddenly, the office door flew open. A table toppled, and a lamp shattered.

Darla had arrived.

CHAPTER 17

Rows and rows of boats lined the harbor. Marlin and Dory swam from stern to stern, trying to find one that looked familiar.

Dory yawned, exhausted. Her eyes fluttered, then closed. She began to sink, falling asleep.

"Dory! Wake up!" Marlin shouted.

Dory opened her eyes. Then she screamed.

A big pelican was swooping toward them. In a flash, he opened his beak and scooped up the two friends.

At the pier, the pelican settled on a dock.

He threw back his head to swallow Marlin and Dory.

"No! I didn't come this far to be breakfast!" Marlin wedged himself sideways in the pelican's mouth.

The pelican made a choking noise. The fish were stuck in his throat.

Farther down the dock, Nigel watched the choking pelican. He flew over to help.

"Fish got your tongue?" he asked.

The pelican opened his mouth. Nigel peered in, then pounded the pelican on the back.

The two fish flew onto the dock.

"I've got to find my son, Nemo!" Marlin cried, gasping for air.

Nigel's eyes opened wide. "He's that fish!" Nigel yelled. "The one that's been fighting the whole ocean!"

Marlin and Dory were flopping down the dock, trying to get back to the water.

"I know where your son is!" Nigel cried.

A flock of curious seagulls suddenly appeared.

The pelican opened his beak. "Hop inside my mouth if you want to live," he said.

"How does that make me live?" Marlin asked, thinking Nigel wanted to eat him.

Nigel shook his head. "No! I know your son. He's orange. He's got a gimpy fin on one side."

Marlin couldn't believe it! This pelican really knew his son. "That's Nemo!" he shouted.

More seagulls swooped down on the dock, surrounding Marlin and Dory.

Nigel dove into the midst of the birds. He snatched the fish from the dock and flew off. Nigel grabbed a mouthful of water from the ocean so that Marlin and Dory could breathe. They were on their way to the dentist's office.

CHAPTER 18

"Hello, Darla," the dentist said. "How's my favorite little niece doing on her special day?"

He placed her in the dentist's chair. "Let's see those pearly whites!" he said, opening her mouth. "Ouch!" he cried as she bit his finger. "Grumpy, are we? I know what you want! You want your present."

"I get a fishy!" Darla shouted.

Looking into the plastic bag, Dr. Sherman knew he didn't have good news for his niece. "Oh, no—poor little guy," he said to himself.

Nemo was floating upside down in the bag.

"He's dead!" the Tank Gang moaned from the tank.

"Must've left your present in the car," the dentist told Darla, trying to hide Nemo. "I'll go get it."

As Dr. Sherman moved the bag behind his back, Nemo opened his eyes.

"He's still alive!" the Tank Gang cheered.

"Why's he playing dead?" one of the fish asked.

The dentist headed toward the bathroom.

"He's gonna get flushed down the toilet!" Gill said happily. "He's gonna get outta here!"

But then the dentist edged over to a trash can.

"Not the trash can!" the Tank Gang cried.

"Hey!" Nigel stuck his beak through the window. "Hey! I found Superfish!"

"Where's Nemo?" Marlin called from inside Nigel's beak. "Where is he?"

"Dentist! Dentist!" the Tank Gang shouted.

"Nigel!" Marlin ordered. "Get in there!" He grabbed Nigel's tongue and, using it like the rudder on a boat, steered him inside.

"What the—" Dr. Sherman said, surprised to see a pelican coming into his office. He lunged for Nigel, but they collided right over Darla where she lay in the dentist's chair.

The dentist dropped the bag onto the dental tray. *Pop!* The bag sprang a slow leak.

With Darla right above him, Nemo continued to play dead.

Nigel and Marlin saw Nemo in the bag— dead. Marlin froze in shock.

"Gotcha!" Dr. Sherman exclaimed. He held Nigel by the beak, keeping it tightly shut.

From inside Nigel's mouth, Marlin yelled, "Nemo!"

Nemo heard his father's voice. "Daddy?" he whispered.

Marlin didn't hear Nemo, and the dentist shoved Nigel out the window.

Gill knew they had to do something—fast. Nemo was running out of air.

"Quick!" Gill shouted. "To the top of Mount Wannahockaloogie!" He motioned for the others to go into action.

In the chair, Darla began to swing Nemo's bag back and forth. "Fishy! Fishy!" she sang.

Nemo was about to pour out through the widening hole in the bag.

In the tank, Bloat lifted a corner of the volcano. Then he inflated himself and nodded to Gill. He had the volcano positioned in just the right way to send Gill in Nemo's direction. Gill swam into the mouth of the volcano.

Jacques turned on the air valve and *whoosh,* Gill was launched into the air. He flew behind Dr. Sherman and landed right on Darla's head.

"Aaagghhh!" Darla screamed.

Nemo fell onto a tray and landed on a dental mirror.

Gill flipped off Darla's head and onto the tray. "Tell your dad I said hi," he said when he spotted Nemo.

Gill smacked the mirror with his tail and sent Nemo sailing into the spit sink.

Nemo slid down the drain.

The dentist saw Nemo just as he was disappearing. "Whoa," he said. Then he picked Gill up off the tray and put him back in the tank.

The gang cheered as Gill entered the tank.

"Is he gonna be okay, Gill?" Gurgle asked.

"Don't worry," Gill said. "All drains lead to the ocean."

111

Nemo tumbled through the drainpipes into the water treatment plant. He slipped around corners and bends. Finally there was a murky light at the end of the tunnel. Nemo reached the end of a drainage pipe on the harbor floor.

"Daddy!" he cried.

CHAPTER 19

High above the harbor, Nigel flew with Marlin and Dory. He landed on the dock and dropped Dory and Marlin back into the water.

"I'm so sorry," Nigel said. "Truly I am."

Marlin gave him a small nod, then swam off with Dory.

"Dory," Marlin said. "If it wasn't for you, I never would have even made it here. So thank you."

Marlin began to swim away.

"Hey, wait a minute. Where are you going?" Dory asked.

"It's over, Dory. We were too late. Nemo's gone. And I'm going home now," Marlin said sadly.

Shocked, Dory pleaded with him. "No, you can't. I remember things better with you. Look—P. Sherman, 42 . . . ohh . . . It's there. I can feel it. I look at you and I'm home. Please, I don't want that to go away. I don't want to forget."

"I'm sorry, Dory," Marlin said. "But I want to forget."

Once again, he swam away and left Dory all alone.

Back at the water treatment plant, two crabs were greedily snatching bits of food from jets of water streaming from holes in the pipe.

The crabs stopped short when Marlin

appeared in the distance. They called out to Marlin, "Hey! Heeeey!"

Marlin paid no attention to them and continued to swim toward the ocean.

"Yeah, that's it, fellah! Just keep on swimming," one crab said. "You got that?"

"Too right, mate," the other crab agreed.

Just then, Nemo popped up from a hole between the two crabs. "Hey! Have you seen my dad?" Nemo asked.

The crabs snapped at Nemo. "Gotcha!" one of the crabs said to Nemo.

"N-n-no!" cried Nemo as he swam away in the direction of the harbor.

CHAPTER 20

Nemo swam aimlessly through the water, calling for his dad. Suddenly, he heard crying and went to find its source.

He found a fish swimming around in circles, mumbling to herself.

"Um, excuse me," Nemo said to the fish. "Are you all right?"

"I don't know where I am. I think I lost somebody, but I can't remember," the fish said.

"It's okay. It's okay," Nemo said, gently taking the fish's fin. "I'm looking for someone, too."

"I'm Dory," Dory said, sniffling.

"I'm Nemo," Nemo said.

"Nemo," Dory said. "That's a nice name."

Together, Nemo and Dory began searching.

"Dad! Dad?" Nemo called out.

"Wait a minute," Dory said. "Is it your dad or my dad?"

"My dad," replied Nemo.

"Got it," said Dory.

"Where are we, anyway?" asked Nemo.

"Hmm," said Dory. She swam over to a sewage pipe and read the logo.

"'Sydney'!" she read.

Suddenly it all came back to her—every bit of her journey with Marlin, and why they had traveled all the way to Sydney.

"Nemo!" she exclaimed, remembering.

"What?" Nemo asked, startled.

"It's you! You're Nemo!" Dory cried.

She held his face tightly in her fins. "You were dead. I saw you! And then here you are. I found you! You're not dead. Your father—"

"You know my father?" Nemo asked excitedly.

Dory didn't answer. She was too busy thinking. Marlin must be by the crabs, she realized. She headed back toward them. Nemo swam right behind her.

In the fishing grounds, Marlin was swimming around aimlessly, sadly thinking he was never going to see his son again.

"Get out of the way!" yelled a grouper.

From above, a giant net was dropping slowly into the ocean.

"Look out!" called another fish. "It's right behind us!"

The groupers raced past Marlin.

"Dad! Dad!" Nemo shouted.

"Nemo?" Marlin said, peering through the murky water.

"Daddy!" called a voice in the distance.

Marlin squinted. He could just make out Nemo—and Dory—swimming toward him. He raced to meet them.

"Look out!" Dory and Nemo screamed.

The net dropped lower, sweeping up fish after fish. Above, a crank on a fishing boat turned, pulling the net toward the surface, but it missed a small swarm of the fish, including Marlin. "Nemo! No!" Marlin cried.

But the net had also missed Nemo. "Dad!" he yelled. They were safe!

"Nemo! Oh, thank goodness!" Marlin exclaimed, hugging his son.

Then they heard a cry for help from the

net. It was Dory! She was caught in the net and it was moving toward the surface.

Nemo looked up at the net and remembered his adventure in the fish tank. "Dad, I know what to do!" he said as he swam toward the net.

Marlin chased after his son. But Nemo had swum between the strands of the net, and Marlin was too big to get through.

"Get out of there! I'm not going to lose you again," Marlin pleaded.

"We have to tell all the fish to swim down together. I know this will work," Nemo assured his father. "Dad, I can do this!"

Marlin realized that all he needed was a little trust and faith in his son. He locked eyes with Nemo. "You're right. I know you can."

They gave each other a high five. "Remember, tell all the fish to swim down," Nemo yelled as he headed toward Dory.

"Well, you heard my son!" shouted Marlin. "Come on! Swim down."

One by one, the groupers stopped to listen. They told other groupers, and soon all the fish in the net began to swim downward.

But the net kept rising. Nemo and Dory were pulled out of the water. They gasped for breath.

"Swim down!" Marlin shouted, this time with more urgency.

The net slowed. For a moment it stayed in place. Then it began to sink.

"It's working!" Nemo yelled. The weight of all the fish swimming down was pulling the net back into the water.

Nemo and Dory pushed their way to the front where they could see Marlin.

"You're doing great, son!" Marlin called.

"Just keep swimming! Just keep swimming!" Marlin and Dory shouted together.

The fish gave one final giant heave as they neared the ocean floor.

Crack! The crank broke. The net sank. Fish poured out, laughing, crying, swimming away as fast as they could. Marlin swam in the opposite direction from the retreating fish.

"Where's Nemo?" he asked Dory.

CHAPTER 21

Marlin and Dory swam around, searching for Nemo. Finally Dory cried, "There!"

Nemo lay buried under the tangled fishing net on the floor of the ocean.

"Nemo!" Marlin gasped as they pushed the heavy net off his son.

Marlin thought back to that horrible day, years ago, when he'd come back to the grotto and discovered only one fish egg left. When he'd promised he would never let anything happen to his one child. His Nemo.

"Nemo?" he pleaded. "Nemo?"

Suddenly, Nemo coughed. "Daddy?"

"Oh, thank goodness." Marlin sighed with relief.

Nemo was alive!

"Dad . . . I'm sorry. I don't hate you," Nemo said.

"Oh, no . . . no. *I'm* sorry, Nemo," Marlin replied. Nemo touched Marlin with his lucky fin, and father and son smiled at what they had accomplished.

"Hey," Marlin said. "Guess what? Sea turtles. I met one. And they live to be a hundred and fifty years old."

"A hundred and fifty?" Nemo replied. "'Cause Sandy Plankton said they only live to be a hundred."

"Sandy Plankton? Do you think I would cross the entire ocean and not know as much as Sandy Plankton?" Marlin said.

Nemo giggled. Then they looked at each other and laughed out loud. They had both been through great adventures and faced many dangers, but it was worth it, now that they were together again.

The morning sun rose over the anemone. It was time for school again. Marlin raced Nemo to school. All the kids were there, starting to climb on Mr. Ray.

"Come aboard, explorers!" Mr. Ray exclaimed.

While Nemo boarded Mr. Ray, Marlin was telling jokes to the other parents.

They all laughed at Marlin's jokes.

Sheldon's dad said, "But seriously, Marty ... did you really do all the things you say you did ... ?"

Just then, three fierce sharks—Bruce, Anchor, and Chum—swam by.

The fish backed away, frightened.

"Don't be alarmed," said Bruce. "We just

wanted to make sure our newest member got home safely."

"Thanks, guys!" Dory swam out from behind the sharks.

"Well, we'll see you next week," Bruce called to Dory. Then he and the other sharks swam away.

"Hold on! Here we go!" Mr. Ray yelled as he started to leave.

"Bye, son! Have fun!" Marlin called to Nemo.

"Bye, Dad!" Nemo cried. "Oh, wait! I forgot something!"

Mr. Ray stopped. Nemo raced over to his dad and gave him a big hug. "Love ya, Dad," he said.

"I love you, too, son," Marlin replied.

Nemo swam back to Mr. Ray and the class left.

"Good-bye," all the kids yelled.

"Bye, Elmo!" called Dory, forgetful as ever.

"Nemo," Marlin said.

"See you after school, Dory! Bye, Dad!" Nemo exclaimed.

"Bye, son." Marlin said. He smiled. Everything was as it should be in the big blue.